I Like Toys

by Maria Velasquez

illustrated by Max Grover

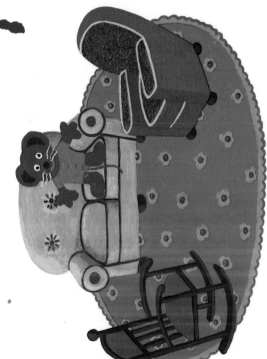

Harcourt

Orlando   Boston   Dallas   Chicago   San Diego

www.harcourtschool.com

I like the house.

 I like the mouse.

I like the coat.

I like the goat.

I like the cat.

I like the mat.

I like the toys.